The Bizzies
Text © 2019 Paula Merlán
Illustrations © 2019 Blanca Millán
This edition © 2019 Cuento de Luz SL
Calle Claveles, 10 | Urb. Monteclaro | Pozuelo de Alarcón | 28223 | Madrid | Spain
www.cuentodeluz.com
Title in Spanish: La familia Uf
English translation by Jon Brokenbrow
Printed in PRC by Shanghai Chenxi Printing Co., Ltd. January 2019, print number 1673-6
ISBN: 978-84-16733-62-0

For Pablo, Álvaro, and Xabi, my delicious Bizzie family.
— Paula Merlán —

For Father P and Elías, my little family P.
— Blanca Millán —

CUENTO
DE LUZ

The BIZZIES

Paula Merlán   Blanca Millán

Mrs. Bizzie is a detective, and she works so hard she never has any free time.

RING-A-DING-DING!

Her alarm clock goes off very early, even on the weekends.

Before she leaves home, she puts minty sweets and an emergency lettuce in her purse in case she gets hungry at work.

Her curly mop of hair conceals a hi-tech magnifying glass, some sunglasses, and a comb, just in case she has a spare moment to brush it.

"I'm working on a really important case!"

That's what she always says when Mr. Bizzie calls her to find out what time she'll be home.

Mr. Bizzie is an adventure photographer. He takes pictures of everything he finds interesting: worms dancing the conga, pirates mowing the lawn, and even a family of chimpanzees playing with bananas.

SAY CHEESE!

That's what he always says when he's about to take a photo.

Bianca Bizzie is their eldest child, and she loves animals. Barkley, the family dog, is her faithful companion. And even though Chucky the Chick lives in the chicken coop, he's still Bianca's greatest friend.

Barnaby Bizzie is younger than Bianca,
and he wants to be a cook when he grows up.
He is very talented, and loves making all sorts
of meals.

Irene, their neighbor, takes care of the Bizzie children until dinnertime, when Mom and Dad come home.

But something strange has been
happening in the Bizzie home lately.
Every day, something different disappears.

"What? You can't find my photo albums?
I'll be right there!" says Mr. Bizzie.

"My telescope isn't there? I'm on my way!"
says Mrs. Bizzie.

"There's something strange going on here,"
they both say.

One afternoon, Bianca and Barnaby accidentally left the door of the chicken coop open.

Chucky peeked out, and ran off as fast as he could. As soon as the children realized what had happened, they told their parents.

"How did it happen?" said Mr. and Mrs. Bizzie.

"We went to see Chucky in the chicken coop, but we forgot to close the door . . ." Bianca sobbed.

"For goodness' sake!" said Mrs. Bizzie. "Something disappears every day! And even though I'm a detective, I'm going to have to call the police so they can solve this mystery!"

Bianca and Barnaby looked at each other with a worried expression. They didn't want to get into trouble with the police.

"Mom, Dad . . ." Barnaby began, "it's our fault that things have been disappearing."

"What? Why?" said their parents, surprised.

"We did it because we wanted you to spend more time with us," said Bianca.

"You always get home really late," said Barnaby, sadly.

"But we didn't mean for Chucky to get lost, said Bianca, with tears in her eyes. "You have to believe us!"

"Come on, stop feeling sorry for yourselves," said Mr. Bizzie. "Let's go and find Chucky!"

Mrs. Bizzie looked in the cookie box, but he wasn't there.

Mr. Bizzie looked in the chicken coop again just to make sure, but he wasn't there either.

Barnaby looked inside his chef's hat, but
there was no sign of the chick.

Even Barkley helped to search.

Bianca began to sing, because Chucky loved music.

"Chucky chicky chick, won't you come back quick?" sang Bianca. But nothing happened.

"Chucky ducky doo, we miss you!" she sang at the top of her voice. But there was no sign of him.

"Come back home where you belong! You've been gone for far too long!" sang Bianca and Barnaby, as loud as they could.

Suddenly they heard a bark. Woof! Woof!

"Barkley! You've found him!" shouted Bianca.

"Good dog," said Barnaby.

Chucky had fallen asleep inside the dog house on a warm, comfy bed he'd made himself out of Barkley's fur.

"Sleepyhead! We were worried about you!" said Bianca. The children were delighted to see their beloved chick again.

"We're so sorry!" said Bianca and Barnaby to their parents. They promised they would never hide anything ever again. The Bizzie family giggled and laughed, and all scrunched up for a huge hug.

From that day on, Mr. and Mrs. Bizzie came home in the afternoon, made dinner together, and read a story to the children before they went to sleep. On Saturdays they would relax at home, and on Sundays they would walk in the park.

"Oh no, Barkley's lost his ball!" said Bianca and Barnaby.

But Mr. and Mrs. Bizzie weren't worried. That mystery would be solved tomorrow!